THIS BOOK
BELONGS TO:

_____

# The *Curious Adventures* of the *Abandoned Toys*

## JULIAN FELLOWES

Based on an idea by SHIRLEY-ANNE LEWIS

Pictures by

## S. D. SCHINDLER

Henry Holt and Company
New York

*To my darling son, Peregrine, who was once*
*the little boy I wrote these stories for*
*—J. F.*

*Thanks to all my visual reference helpers:*
*Susan, Leslie, Julian, Julia, Noa, Liz, Ann, and Robyn*
*—S. D. S.*

Henry Holt and Company, LLC
*Publishers since 1866*
175 Fifth Avenue
New York, New York 10010
www.henryholtchildrensbooks.com

Henry Holt® is a registered trademark of Henry Holt and Company, LLC.
Text copyright © 2007 by Julian Fellowes
Illustrations copyright © 2007 by S. D. Schindler
All rights reserved.
Distributed in Canada by H. B. Fenn and Company Ltd.

Library of Congress Cataloging-in-Publication Data
Fellowes, Julian.
The curious adventures of the abandoned toys / by Julian Fellowes;
based on an idea by Shirley-Anne Lewis; pictures by S. D. Schindler.—1st ed.
p.    cm.
Summary: When Doc the bear arrives at the dump from his former home, he isn't sure about
what awaits him but his new friends are determined to make his new home a welcoming one.
ISBN-13: 978-0-8050-7526-7 / ISBN-10: 0-8050-7526-7
[1. Teddy bears—Fiction.  2. Toys—Fiction.]  I. Lewis, Shirley-Anne.  II. Schindler, S. D., ill.  III. Title.
PZ7.F33587Cur 2007    [E]—dc22    2006031375

First Edition—2007 / Designed by Patrick Collins
The artist used ink on watercolor paper to create the art for this book.
Printed in China on acid-free paper. ∞

1  3  5  7  9  10  8  6  4  2

# Contents

## PART ONE

# The Abandoned Toys

It was a dull day in early March, and the dayroom of the children's ward in Deerhurst Hospital looked even more dilapidated than usual. The walls must once have been a cheerful pink but they had faded to the color of cough medicine. A large, scratched table was surrounded by some uncomfortable-looking chairs, a cupboard full of jigsaws (most of which were missing one vital piece), and a battered laundry basket, without its lid, stood in the corner near the window. Here lived what the nurses referred to as the "cuddly toys," although there was an element of impertinence in this which most of the occupants of the basket found rather irritating. These consisted of several stuffed seals, some rag dolls, a monkey or two, a kangaroo with an empty pouch and a variety of teddy bears in differing states of repair. The largest bear was made of brown artificial fur and he had been bought at an expensive toy shop by a rich benefactor's niece while she and her uncle were driving to the opening of the new ward.

The bear originally stood in a colorful box labeled "Doctor Bear," with plenty of packing and a cellophane window to see out of. Inside it, the bear had worn a white coat with a stethoscope round his neck and a reflector on his head. In his paw he held a small, plastic thermometer. When he was first carried into the warm, leather-smelling interior of the benefactor's car, he had looked forward to many happy years in a smart nursery. But he had not traveled for more than a few minutes before he realized that he had not been bought as a toy for the child herself. She was to present him to the hospital at the ceremony, where her uncle was to cut the ribbon at the door of the new building. It had been a blow, one might as well admit it. From his first

moments on the factory assembly line to his final hour in the store, Doc (for so he had christened himself, although the children did not know it) had been taught to expect the love of a single, special child. He was, after all, an exceptionally warm-hearted bear. But in time he came to accept his fate, for while he had never figured as the key toy in any childhood, he'd nevertheless featured in the dreams and dramas of many. He had seen parents cry with relief as their boy or girl took the first faltering steps after a dangerous illness; he had soothed some children, nervous before their operations, and diverted others as they waited for parents coming to take them home. Once a young father, tears pouring down his cheeks, had held him close and begged to keep him "as a memento" and the nurse had shaken her head and said "better not" and put him gently back into the basket.

All in all, he had seen a good deal of life, despite his confinement to the dayroom. He had lost his coat and the thermometer and the reflecting mirror, all mislaid over the years in the course of various games (although, oddly, the stethoscope had survived). One ear had been torn off and sewn back inexpertly with some blue wool by a child seamstress more enthusiastic than gifted. Even so, he had the satisfaction of knowing that his career thus far had been not merely interesting but useful.

"No one is indispensable," he would say with a throaty chuckle to the childless kangaroo, when in his heart he thought he came as near to being indispensable as anyone could be.

He was quite wrong.

On the March morning in question, he received the first

intimations of mortality. One of the senior nurses, whom the toys knew well, opened the door and ushered in two strangers: a young man in a baggy linen suit and a woman in glasses, carrying a large briefcase. They stopped and stood in the center of the room, looking about them in silence for a moment.

"Oh, dear," said the woman in a harsh, London accent. The man nodded.

"Well," he said, "we've got our work cut out here, and no mistake."

The nurse looked rather pained. "But it's only for one quick visit. Surely if we just spruce it up a little . . . ?" At the look in the visitors' eyes, she faltered.

"One quick visit that will be covered by the national press and several magazines and is scheduled for six pages in *Hello*? No. I do not think we can just spruce it up a little." The woman approached the toy basket. Reaching down, she seized hold of Doc's arm and pulled him out of the pile. "I mean, just look." She pulled his ear back to show the blue wool darning and then cast him down again.

The nurse bristled. "The children are very fond of the old toys," she said. "They like them better than the new ones."

"Do they?" The woman winked at her companion. "I don't think so." Before the nurse could speak again, the woman smiled and said briskly, "Don't worry. It won't cost anything. We'll find some manufacturers to donate whatever we need. Then we can get the Duchess to pose near the basket. They'll be delighted." She switched her attention to the sofa and the curtains.

The young man in the strange suit was perhaps the kinder of the two. He spoke gently to the nurse when his companion's back was turned. "We'll just put some of them away, that's all. You can get them out again when it's over." And maybe that had been the plan. But it was not what happened.

First the dayroom was closed and the toys were dragged into a cupboard in the corridor, where they stayed for four or five stuffy and airless days. By the end of this time, the dolls and the monkeys were growing seriously depressed.

"I've never been lucky," said the kangaroo with the empty pouch. "Nothing's ever gone right for me since I was first cut out."

On the fifth day, the cupboard was opened and a couple of workmen seized the basket and dragged it into the light. The toys had some difficulty controlling their blinking, but the rule that a toy must not move in sight of a human is an absolute one and, in a strange way, it helped to steady their nerves as they were pulled down the corridor and back into the dayroom, where the young man in the loose suit and his companion awaited them.

There had been a transformation. The walls were a soft shade of apricot, and thick gingham curtains stood sentinel at every window. But the real surprise was in the corner. There, where the hamper had always stood in the past, was a large red plastic container. It was more than half full of gleaming, brand-new toys. Robots, Bionicles, Barbie dolls and replicas of cartoon characters stared smugly across at the tattered contents of the ancient basket. "Our paint is unchipped," they seemed to say. "Our batteries are new, our voice boxes are in working order. How can you hope to compete with us?" Doc even thought he heard the faint echo of a sneering laugh coming from the direction of Barbie's boyfriend, Ken.

"Right. Tip it up," said the woman, and the next moment the toys were lying, higgledy-piggledy, in a scattered heap on the floor. The adults approached, and so began the terrible choice. Some dolls got through, and almost all the monkeys and four of

the bears, one quite old, were snatched up and tossed in among the shining novelties. But there were shocks. Not one of the seals was chosen, nor was a highwayman rabbit who had never entertained the faintest notion that he wouldn't be part of the new regime. He was so stunned that he nearly spoke. It was only Doc's tweak at his arm that brought him to his senses.

Then again, not all the surprises were bad. "Oh, look!" said the woman, pulling the childless kangaroo out of the pile. "Just what we need!" And from somewhere in the new box she produced a motherless baby and pushed it into the empty pouch. Doc never saw the kangaroo again, but he would always remember how, in a single second, happiness lit up her mournful features so brilliantly that he was afraid the humans would notice. He risked a wink, and her glass eyes moistened as she gave a tiny, contented nod. Then she too vanished into the red box.

The woman stepped back. "That's it, I think." She glanced over to the friendly nurse. "The administrator thinks we should

give them away in the hall. Good for public relations, and really, we've got so many new ones." And the nurse nodded rather wistfully and said that, yes, she supposed it was more sensible. With a quick stroke of his darned ear, she parted from Doc forever.

Then the basket stood in the hall for a long, terrible day with a large, handwritten sign saying FREE TOYS. ONE PER CHILD. Boys and girls had leaned in, hour after painful and insulting hour, plucking out the lucky ones. The highwayman rabbit went quickly, proving, as he whispered hastily to Doc, that he should never have been discarded in the first place. The seals were taken, the monkeys, the remaining dolls, until at last no one was left in the dusty basket except for Doc and a small squirrel made out of dirty red flannel. Now it was nighttime, and the hall of the hospital was almost empty. Empty enough, anyway, to chance a little conversation.

"Well," said the squirrel, "all I can say is what a day!" His voice carried a slight West Country burr.

"It has been rather draining," agreed Doc.

"We ought to make a joke out of why we haven't been chosen," said the squirrel, "but I'm past joking, really."

"It's sad for you," said Doc, in a kindly voice. "But I suppose I'm a bit too old to be taken on as a new toy, so to speak." He gave his voice a humorous lilt, but as he spoke it dawned on him, perhaps for the first time, that his words were true. That his working life as a toy was finished. It was a sobering thought. The squirrel made a sign with his eyes, and they were both still. An old man in janitor's dungarees looked down on them. He was joined by a younger companion.

"Grab ahold, Tom," said the older man, and together they wheeled the basket away.

Doc had never seen a basement. It seemed a strange and terrible place. Pipes chugged and glugged from wall to ceiling and roaring away at the far end were the boilers. Slowly the basket was wheeled towards the heat coming from the furnaces. Doc could feel his heart start to beat violently, and the red squirrel let out a squeal that was drowned by the noise of the wheels.

"I don't know," said the younger man, looking down, "This one'd be all right with a bit of a wash. I think I'll take it for my youngest. She loves squirrels." He leaned in, and a second later the squirrel had gone to a new life.

Doc was alone. He did not wish the squirrel any harm but could not resist a tinge of regret that the janitor's daughter had not instead had a preference for bears. The older man reached down and seized his leg.

For a moment Doc hung there upside down as Tom started to wrestle with the heavy fastenings of the furnace door. With a murmured prayer to the Great Bear, he steadied his nerves and waited.

"Drat this thing," said Tom. "I can't budge it."

The older man shook his head. "Where's the point for a single bear? Just chuck him in the dustbin and have done with it."

With a grunt, Tom nodded and strode towards a door in the corner while Doc swung along by his side. With a cool gust of night air, Doc found himself suspended in an alley. Large industrial bins stood against the wall of the hospital. Tom hurled the bear into the nearest one and turned back inside.

It was a dark evening, and there was a slight drizzle that soon soaked his fur, but as he lay on top of the rubbish Doc could not resist a sense of elation. He felt, as he wriggled beneath some surgical wadding and a copy of the *Guardian* and settled down to sleep, that, all things considered, he had withstood his testing with an admirable lack of panic.

"'Allo, 'allo, what's that round 'is neck?"

"A steffoscope. What'ja fink? It's an 'ospital, innit?"

The laughter of the men showed that there was nothing hostile in this exchange but even so it was startling for Doc to wake in the hands of a complete stranger dressed in overalls and smelling of litter. Soon, however, he was congratulating himself that he was not still in the bin, which he now saw had been gripped by a pair of mechanical arms attached to the rear of a vast garbage truck parked at the mouth of the alley. With an almighty roar, the bin was tipped up, shedding its contents into a black hole lined with serrated metal teeth. At the touch of a switch, the teeth began to gurgle and chew. Doc could barely suppress a shudder as he was carried round to the front of the vehicle. There against the grille hung several strings. One of these was fastened round Doc's waist and in another minute, he was swinging at the front of the garbage truck as it set off down the road.

Despite the Shock of the New, he spent quite an interesting day—certainly a vast improvement on the shame and terror that had colored the previous week. Although it did strike Doc, as he jangled and jumped against the warm grille, that it might be a lonely life for a bear if he was simply to hang here alone in the wind and the rain for the foreseeable future. At last the truck finished its round and set off past the edge of the town. By a gap in a high hedge, Doc was just able to read the sign DEERHURST REFUSE DEPOSIT before the vehicle turned in. It passed up a long drive to a courtyard where the rubbish was noisily unloaded and then, with a series of cheery good-byes, the men went off for the day and a great silence descended on the yard.

Doc hung there.

After an hour or two he did risk a slight look to the right and left, but all he could see were other trucks, some low and rather ugly office buildings and beyond, a seemingly endless pile of rubbish that spread out through the surrounding fields, over hillocks, filling dells, wrapping and engulfing bushes and trees. It would be a lie to pretend that he was cheered at the sight, but he was not a neurotic bear. The thought of spending his life hanging at the front of a rubbish truck was not enticing, but it was so vast an improvement on his prospects at the mouth of the furnace twenty-four hours earlier that he would not allow himself to be depressed. Instead, he dozed off.

When he woke up, it was pitch dark. At first he could not fathom what had drawn him out of his dream but then he heard a small voice coming from below.

"Bear," it said, "wouldn't you like to get down?" And, as his eyes adjusted to the gloom, Doc was able at last to make out the shapes of not one but two small teddy bears staring up at him.

"Can I?" he said, surprised at the reckless danger in the suggestion.

They nodded. "They never remember which toys were at the front. It's quite safe."

Doc nodded. He fiddled with the string and as soon as the

knot was untied, he fell, bouncing off the bumper into the dirt. There he found himself looking up at the two visitors. One was small and blue, a baby's teddy, really—not, he thought, the type to inspire life-long nostalgia (he would ever after feel silently guilty about this first impression)—and the other was pale brown and furry like himself, if rather smaller. This bear did look as if someone had been fond of it. There was a large chintz patch on its rear and one of the ears had been darned in unmatching brown wool.

"Are you all right?" inquired the blue bear gently.

"I think so," said Doc, standing up and brushing himself off a bit. He looked around nervously. "I suppose this is—I mean, no one's going to see us here, are they?"

"Heavens, no," said the brown bear with the patch. "They won't be back for hours."

"Good," said Doc. It was very different from the hospital, where, what with night shifts and early morning tea and emergencies and everything, there was really no such thing as a "safe" time.

"I expect this is all rather a shock," said the blue bear. "It usually is. But you mustn't worry."

"You probably feel that your owner has made a ghastly mistake and you shouldn't be here. Most toys do." The brown bear smiled encouragingly.

Doc shook his head. "No. I wouldn't say that. In one way I suppose I shouldn't be here, but that's only because they were going to throw me into a furnace. They couldn't get the door open," he finished lamely.

"Heavens alive." The blue bear sat down on an overturned boot, steadying herself with one paw.

Doc shook his head again. "Please don't let me upset you," he said. "I was just trying to explain that, on the whole, I am not as sorry to find myself here as most toys must be."

The brown bear nodded. "Well, it is hard for them to accept that they aren't needed anymore. You know how it is. It wasn't too bad for me. I was in an orphanage that was closed down. I mean, in such a case, there's no sense of personal failure. It's just happened and one has to get on with things. I feel for the toys who are tossed out by their own children. I've heard some very sad stories."

The blue bear nodded. "Cora, for a start." But she was silenced by a look from her companion, who turned back to Doc.

"You must allow me to make the introductions. I'm Humphrey and this is Nell."

Doc nodded. "I'm Doc," he said, indicating his stethoscope which, by some miracle, had survived the buffetings of the day. He smiled at Nell. "Where are you from?" he asked. It was Humphrey who answered.

"The thing is, Doc . . . ," he coughed slightly, ". . . one isn't supposed to ask that question around here. If a toy wants to tell you how he or she wound up in a dustbin, all well and good, but you can't ask. Do you see?" He smiled to take the rebuke out of his words.

"Humphrey's right," said Nell. "But you mustn't think I mind at all. I fell out of a pram on a crossing. I was quite lucky I wasn't squashed flat by a truck, but somehow I got kicked into the gutter, swept up and here I am."

"How wretched," said Doc.

"Not really. My boy was only four months old and, if I'm honest, they're not very rewarding at that age. I spent most of my working life being flung out of prams or cots, and besides, we baby toys don't have the same career expectations as you lot. We're almost always thrown away before the child has much of a say in it. The fact is I'm rather happy here and I hope you will be, too."

"You can stay with me tonight," said Humphrey, "and tomorrow we can look about for something more permanent."

Humphrey's home turned out to be one of those tin bread bins where the whole side lifts up and over, like a mini garage door. It was quite large but even so, once Doc had stretched out head to toe with Humphrey, it did seem a little, well, full. The day had been exhausting and before long Doc was in a deep sleep, but it was no great surprise that his host suggested, almost as soon as he had opened his eyes the next morning, that they set off in search of a new home. "It'd be nice to settle that before you come and meet the others," said Humphrey.

"What others?"

"Well, there's an owl called the General whom you ought to pay a call on. He's a dear old boy but he likes the forms to be observed. You know. And . . ."

"And?"

"Well, I suppose you should meet Cora. . . ." Humphrey fell silent without further explanation. This was the second time Doc had heard the name.

"Who is Cora?"

Humphrey waved his arms in a vague manner. "Oh, a doll. Just a doll," he said breezily. "But it's always good to start off in people's good books." Before Doc could answer this, Humphrey was pointing at what looked like a brand-new orange-box, brilliantly colored images of foreign fruit still clinging to its sides. It was quite large, almost a crate really, and had the great merit of being divided into two separate compartments. "Isn't this just the thing? On its side, with some plywood to shield the entrance? Two rooms? What could be better?"

Doc had spent his entire working life jammed hugger-mugger into a basket with a very disparate group of toys and now he thought he might enjoy a little solitude. He nodded. "I wonder if we might drag it down there. Beneath that tree." He pointed with his paw to a sheltered spot beneath a beech tree. Humphrey nodded, and half an hour later, Doc was a Bear of Property.

Nell was waiting for them by the General's khaki knapsack. It did not look frightfully dry, but as Humphrey explained, it was the only bit of military rubbish on the dump and the General had been determined to have it. He kept a large cake tin near for really wet nights.

"I suppose I mustn't ask him how he came to be here?" said Doc as they walked towards the blue bear.

"Certainly not," said Humphrey, "though he's bound to tell you. In his case, it really was a mistake, you see. His little boy lost him in a railway station."

"How sad," said Doc.

"It is sad," said Humphrey with a nod, "but, to my mind, not as sad as being thrown out."

"I suppose not," said Doc.

They were distracted by Nell, who was hurrying towards them. "He isn't here!" she shouted. "There's been some sort of drama. He's over at Cora's."

"Who told you?"

"One of the rats."

Humphrey snorted. "They always exaggerate."

"Shall we go to Cora's, then?" asked Doc. There was something so strange and wonderful to him about this new life of free movement and talk, far from prying human eyes, that he felt game for anything.

"I suppose so," said Humphrey, with markedly diminished enthusiasm. "And, by the way, she's Lady Cora to you."

"And to you," said Nell.

Lady Cora lived in a large, round hatbox from Harrods. It was green with a yellow satin bow from a discarded flower arrangement fixed onto it. As the toys approached, they could see the lid was open and the doll was standing among the folds of lavender tissue inside, her china hands resting on the edge of the cardboard, like someone in a box at the opera. At first sight, her costume was a curious one. She wore a tartan skirt, a lamé evening jacket, a feather boa and on her porcelain head a turban made of what looked suspiciously like a red paper napkin, which she tossed this way and that.

"What is the matter with her head?" Doc asked Nell.

"She always does that," said Nell. "I think in her mind she's tossing her shining curls. But they've all gone." By this time she was whispering, as they were quite near the box although they could not yet see what was holding the doll's attention. Another toy, this one a stuffed, woolen owl, also appeared to be deep in concentration, although it was still not clear on what. At the sound of their approach, he turned, giving Doc rather a shock. The owl's bandaged leg, darned wing, and above all, the black patch replacing one eye conspired to give him a somewhat alarming appearance.

"Hello," said Nell. "This is Doc. He's a newcomer and we thought he ought to meet you both."

The owl nodded towards the bear in a distracted fashion, but the doll let out a sharp scream. "Take him away!" she shrieked. "There's too much going on this morning! I will not be pestered by strangers!"

Doc stepped forward. "Lady Cora," he said. It was at once clear that this mode of address had a mollifying effect. The turban inclined towards the bear. Doc continued. "I should hate to feel that I pressed myself on you at an inopportune moment. I am a new arrival, and as such, it was felt that I should lose no

time in calling on you. That has been done. I will now retire and return at a more convenient hour."

The turban actually nodded gracefully. "Bear," said the doll, "you see me now living like a wild thing in the desert, but it was not always thus. You must not think I do not know good manners when I see them. I have sat on the lap of my child in the company of kings. Ministers have stroked my hair, princesses have praised my clothes—"

"Yes, yes, Cora," said the owl. "So you have told us many times, but just now we have a problem." The others walked over to where he was standing and it was suddenly quite clear what the difficulty was. A large blackbird was sitting in a dell just below the hatbox. One of its wings was spread out across the grass. It was whimpering.

"Can you tell me again where it hurts exactly?" The owl attempted to be kind, but he could not avoid a certain military crispness in his tone.

"Where do you think? In the wing!" it answered sharply.

The other toys gathered round the bird. Cora, rather than be left behind in her box, climbed out and joined them. Doc was able to see that the final detail of her oddly ill-matched ensemble was a pair of riding boots. She noticed his stare and gave him a conspiratorial smile. "If one's going to have a 'country adventure' one might as well be dressed for it," she said with a gay laugh.

"She hasn't got anything else to wear," whispered Humphrey. "That's all she had with her when she was thrown away." Cora glared at him.

The blackbird spoke again. "I do not mean to sound ungrateful, but if none of you are going to offer any help, I would rather not be an object of curiosity."

"Hold on, old chap," said the owl. "We will be of help just as soon as I've decided on a plan."

"I wonder—" Doc started, but the owl silenced him with an impatient flick of his wing. "Please," he said, "I'm trying to think."

"It's just—"

"Do be quiet," said Cora. "You don't yet know the General's ways."

"Ho hum, it's a puzzle, and no mistake." The General drummed his woolen feathers across his tummy.

"Permission to speak, sir!"

This time the owl looked approvingly at the bear. It was not in him to refuse a request so worded, and he nodded his head.

Doc ignored Cora's audible sigh. "I have spent much of my

life working in a hospital and I think I may have some ideas," said the bear, adding "Sir!" at the end for good measure. He advanced towards the bird and began to run his paws along the length of the wing.

The owl watched with interest, and so did the two smaller bears, but Cora, who was never very happy when someone else was holding center stage, crossed her arms and muttered, "I hate showing off," to no one in particular.

"It isn't broken," said Doc to the blackbird.

"Are you sure?" answered the bird in such a different tone from before that it was clear to the surrounding toys that he had been under the most intolerable strain.

"Quite sure. It is dislocated. Here. Did you strike a branch or do something out of the ordinary when you took off this morning?"

"As a matter of fact, I misjudged the height of a hedge. How clever you are. But what happens now?"

Doc beckoned the others down to join him. "If the General could steady him from the other side? Then Humphrey and Lady Cora and I will push when I say 'now.'"

"What about me?" said Nell.

"You stand by his head and cheer him up."

"I'll be perfectly all right," said the bird, but when the little blue teddy came round and touched his beak, he did not ask her to leave.

"Push! I am to push? With my hands? Really!"

"Yes, Cora," said the owl firmly. "You are to push."

Doc felt among the feathers in silence for a few more

moments as they got into position, then, when they were quite ready, he shouted "Now!" All the toys flung their weight against the blackbird, who let out a terrific squeak right into Nell's ear.

"Why don't we break his legs while we're at it?" said Cora.

But the bird, after his initial shock, seemed to feel that something had indeed taken place. Very tentatively, he folded his wing. "By Jove, you've done it!" he said.

"Go easy with it for a few days," said Doc. "No more hedge-skimming for a while."

"No indeed," said the blackbird. He was standing, both wings in place, hesitating. "You must let me know if I can ever do anything for you."

"Off you go," said Doc gently.

"Well, the thing is, I am rather late—"

"Carefully, mind," said Doc, and in another moment the bird was wheeling above their heads. With a last called good-bye, he was gone.

"I don't think there was anything wrong with him at all," said Cora, rubbing her arms with a groan. "As for me, I doubt I'll ever use my hands again. I'm in agony." She swung her legs over the side of the box with a shrill scream and fell into the lavender tissue paper, carefully arranging her position becomingly as she did so. She opened one eye to assess the effect, but the others ignored her and gathered round the bear to pat him on the back.

"You mustn't mind Cora," said the General as he escorted Doc back to the orange-box later that day. "She was thrown out by her child. The child of the dazzling social connections that she bores us with night and noon chucked out Cora after years of service." He paused for a moment. "Wasn't even a maid or a nanny. The girl put her in the bin herself. Poor old Cora blanks it out, even now. Can't deal with it at all. And no wonder. That never happened to me."

"I know," said Doc. "Your boy loved you. He never would have parted with you willingly. You'd be with him today."

The owl stopped and looked at him gratefully, his one glass eye misting over slightly. "I believe I would," he muttered. His voice had gone rather gravelly, and he seemed for a moment to look into the distance to someplace far away. "Of course he'd be growing up by now . . . but, even so, I'm pretty sure we'd be together still." And with that, he tucked his wing beneath the bear's arm as they strolled towards Doc's new home beneath the beech tree in a clearing in the rubbish.

## PART TWO

# The Rabbit Who Was
# Thrown Away by Accident

It was a bright summer day in the middle of June and even in
the rubbish dump the air felt fresher and the sky bluer than it
had in months. Weeds were springing up green and bright, and
wildflowers had started to appear between the piles of boxes and
bags. Even the rats seemed to be taking things easier and looked
less shifty than usual as they ran about their business. Doc
opened his eyes and looked around his neat and ordered orange-
box with calm satisfaction. He got up and adjusted his
stethoscope, then he scratched his ear, checked that the darning
wasn't getting any looser, and set off in search of Humphrey.

He found him sitting in the sunshine in front of the old
leather briefcase where Nell lived. Nearby, on a clear patch of
grass, the little blue bear was busy playing skittles with some
wooden cotton spools and an old rubber ball. It wasn't a very
good game, as the spools were too broad to be knocked down,
even when they were hit, so Humphrey was calling out the score
instead. "Three!" he cried. And then, "Four!" And so on.

Doc watched for a while. "Wouldn't it be better with something that would fall over?" he said at last.

Nell shook her head. "It wouldn't be such fun for Humphrey." She smiled.

Doc gestured with one paw at the blue sky overhead. "I thought we might ride on the truck."

Nell stopped throwing. "Yes, let's." She nodded to Humphrey, who stood up, dusting off the chintz patch on his rear. "What about the others?" said Nell.

"We could ask the General," said Doc.

"And Cora," said Nell firmly.

"And Cora," answered Doc meekly. So they set off to find them.

The General was perched on the highest pile of black bags in the dump, giving a carefully studied impression of an old, discarded toy. At the sound of their calls, he silenced them with a flick of his wing. "Don't break my cover!" he whispered urgently.

Nell climbed up the mound. "We're going on the truck," she said. "We wondered if you'd like to come with us."

The General shook his head, scarcely moving it as he did so. "Don't think I'd better, old girl," he muttered softly with a conspiratorial wink. "I may be onto something here, so I'm going to keep watch for a while. Let me know if you see anything suspicious on your rounds. Can't be too careful. Keep mum, she's not so dumb. Know what I mean?" He winked again and resumed his lookout pose.

"Dear old General," said Nell softly, tucking in a stray bit of the bandage round the owl's leg. She clambered down to the others at the bottom. "He can't come. Military duties," she said with a smile, and this time it was she who winked as they set off again.

Before long they were outside Cora's hatbox. The doll had placed it in the shade of a large syringa bush and the sweet scent of the white blossoms filled the air.

Doc sighed. "She'll be asleep," he said. "She won't want to be woken." He exchanged an eye-rolling shrug with Humphrey.

Nell ignored them and, lifting the lid as carefully as she could, stuck her head inside. "Cora?" she said softly.

After a moment, a shrill voice answered from the depths of the lavender tissue paper. "Lady Cora to you!" Which was followed by a loud groan. "Put that light out!" Gradually the fragrant wrapping parted, and at last the painted porcelain face emerged, blinking in horror at the sunlight. She focused on Nell. "Oh," she said, "it's you." Cora was still in her sleeping turban and was holding what appeared to be a small ice-pack to her china temples. It contained no ice, of course, but it made her feel better all the same. She stepped gingerly down onto the ground.

"It's such a lovely day," said Nell. "We thought we'd go for a ride on the truck and we wondered if you'd like to come with us."

Cora snorted, pulling at the end of a lace curtain and draping it about her like a peignoir. She tilted her head.

Doc and Humphrey watched in silence. This performance was not new to them.

"When?" she asked.

"Now," said Doc.

"Now?" shrieked the doll. "Before I've had time to dress! Are you mad? I haven't decided what to wear!"

"Come on, Cora," said Doc wearily. "You've only got one set of clothes. If you want to come, just put them on."

"I will not!" said Cora. "And for your information, bear, it isn't what you wear—it's how you wear it!" She tossed her turban and, retreating to the hatbox, pulled the lid down firmly.

Doc nodded. "That's that," he said. "Let's go."

Nell shook her head. "You shouldn't have said that about the clothes."

"Why not? It's true."

"It's true, but it isn't kind."

Doc gave a sort of *hrrumph!* noise in his throat, but he was silent otherwise. For in his heart he agreed with Nell. He was a generous bear, when all was said and done, and he did not like to hurt.

It was not long before the three teddies reached the yard where the garbage trucks were parked. They were early so as to be in place when the men arrived. They climbed onto the front bumper of the nearest truck, fastened the loose strings around their middles, and settled down patiently to wait. Before long all three were snoozing, and it was only the sound of the motor that woke them.

They traveled at first down narrow, leafy lanes where the breeze blew in their faces and ruffled their fur as they swayed on their bouncing strings. Every so often, the truck would stop and the men would jump down to collect the rubbish and hurl it into the cavernous opening at the rear, and the teddies would listen to the chilling sound of the great metal mouth as it chewed and swallowed the load. Then the men would call to each other, jump back onto the truck, and be off again.

At last they turned into the main square of the little town. There had been a market the day before, and there was a good deal of rubbish to be cleared. The toys watched silently, basking in the sun, as the team bustled about, scooping up the debris left over from the many stalls until one of the men came to the front of the cab carrying something. He reached for an empty string between Doc and Nell and tied it round what they could now see was a small gray toy rabbit. There was a call from the back of the truck: "Fancy some tea, Ned?" The man nodded and set off with the others for a café on the far side of the square, leaving the toys in peace.

With the faintest of movements, the teddies looked at their new companion. The rabbit was old and threadbare, and one of his glass eyes appeared to be a replacement. An unusual detail was the pair of silver plastic spectacles perched on the end of his nose. For a while he dangled there in silence until at last the others heard him utter a low moan, "Oh, dear," and as they watched, a tiny tear formed in the older of the two eyes and trickled underneath the spectacles to the end of the nose, where it hung for a moment before splashing onto the bumper below.

"Don't worry," whispered Doc. "It'll be all right." He knew there was always a period of adjustment before a newly discarded

toy could start to think straight. These things could not be hurried.

The rabbit looked up. His gaze was almost blank, but then it focused on the face of the kindly bear. "You don't understand." He spoke in a barely audible breath. "There's been a terrible mistake."

Doc nodded. "There, there," he said. "I'm sure there has." He thought that if he had sixpence for every time he'd heard that, he'd be the richest bear in the kingdom. But there was no time for further discussion, as the men returned. The motor started up again, and they were off on the rest of the rounds.

Back at the rubbish dump, once the men had gone home, the teddies started to untie themselves. The rabbit, who had not spoken since they left the market square, watched them with surprise. "Don't we have to stay here?" he said. "I thought toys weren't allowed to move if there was any chance of humans noticing."

"They don't notice," said Humphrey. "There are so many of them. They always think one of the others has done it. It's quite safe. Come on."

So the rabbit undid the string (which was a relief as the man had tied it rather tight) and climbed down. "What happens now?" he said.

"You'd better come and meet the General and Cora," said Doc. "And perhaps then you can tell us your story." Together they set off across the piles of rubbish.

Cora was up by this time and dressed, as Doc had predicted, in her usual tartan skirt and lamé jacket set off by her vivid paper-napkin turban. It looked rather a warm outfit for such a sunny day, but Cora did not appear to mind. She was sitting on her hatbox, legs crossed, squeezing some blackberry juice onto her nails.

"This is Cora," said Doc. The doll threw him a frosty look.

"Lady Cora," said Nell.

The rabbit stepped forward and gave a slight bow. "Your ladyship," he said.

Cora brightened. Tossing away the remains of the squashed berry, she smiled at the newcomer. "And who are you?" she asked.

"My name is Augustus, and though I do not wish to seem discourteous, I must tell you that a terrible mistake has been made. I should not be here."

Cora nodded with the practiced wisdom of a Doll Who Has Seen Life. "We are all the victims of such mistakes here," she said. "How can it be anything but a mistake when a lifetime's service is rewarded with a short flight through the air and a dustbin at the end of it? My advice to you, Augustus, and to every toy is this: Live life to the full and, above all, don't look back." She sighed and dabbed her dry eyes.

The rabbit shook his head. "You don't understand. There has really been a mistake. My family and I have been living in the white corner house in the square. Do you know it?" The others nodded. They knew every house in the town. "We are moving, and the mother of my boy, George, put two boxes into his room: one for rubbish and one for toys that were to go to the new house. Unfortunately, his aunt, a fearfully stupid woman it must

be said, was helping him. When the time came she took the wrong box down to the front door. All the rubbish has gone to the new home and all his favorite games, his model engine, and I have ended up here."

The teddies and even Cora were silent. This did seem to be a mistake indeed. A genuine mistake. The rabbit and his boy had truly been separated by accident.

At this moment they were interrupted by the husky tones of the General, who arrived, as he always did, flapping his wings as if he had flown in. "What's going on here? All present and correct? Who's this?" He pointed a woolly feather at Augustus. "A new recruit? Don't worry. We'll show you the ropes in no time."

Doc introduced the owl and told him Augustus's story. The General nodded sagely.

Doc knew that the owl had the distinction among the toys of being the only one of them (until Augustus, that is) who had been separated from his child by accident. He had not been thrown out but lost in a railroad station when he had slipped off the seat they had been sitting on and fallen behind a litter bin. From this low angle, he had caught a last glimpse of his boy searching the empty platform, tears pouring down his face, as the train pulled inexorably away. Naturally, the rabbit's tale awakened the memory afresh and the General was forced to turn aside for a moment and clear his throat. The rest of the toys were silent until he was ready to speak.

"Unlike these others," said the owl at last, "I was not thrown away on purpose either."

Cora wriggled uncomfortably and rather regretted discarding

the blackberry. She thought this reminder of her pain lacking in taste.

The owl continued. "You are the victim of a mistake, a mischance, as I was. Mine was irremediable. Yours may not be." Doc looked at Humphrey, Nell looked at Cora. But the General was just getting into his stride. "First, I must know when your family is leaving the present house."

"Today," said the rabbit with the trace of a stammer. He was slightly disconcerted by the black patch over the General's left eye.

The owl nodded. "Oh. That, I must admit, is a setback. In the square, it would have been easy enough to let you fall from the truck at the foot of the steps of your home. Never mind. On to Plan B. Where exactly are they moving?"

"I don't know," said the rabbit.

After this there was a deeper silence than before. It was again the owl who spoke first. "Ah," he said. "That is a real disadvantage. There is no point in hiding from it."

Cora let out a low, bitter laugh. The hopelessness of the

rabbit's situation had restored her spirits. "Augustus, darling." She stretched out to her arms to him. The rabbit looked rather nervous and took a step backward. "Sometimes in life you just have to be terribly, terribly brave. *C'est la guerre!* Look at me! You wouldn't guess that my heart was in a thousand pieces, would you? I've cried a river, Augustus, believe me, a river." She paused and attempted, unsuccessfully, to make her porcelain lip tremble.

"Do be quiet, Cora," said Humphrey. "The General's thinking."

"Thank you, Humphrey," said the owl. "I am thinking, and I believe I have come up with a solution." The teddies, the doll and the rabbit leaned in expectantly. "But first, we must ascertain where the family has gone. Only then will we know the size of the problem."

"But how can we?" said Nell.

"By searching their rubbish," said the owl. "I cannot believe that we will not find some indication of the new address if we look hard enough."

Doc nodded with undisguised approval.

Humphrey sidled up next to him. "I suppose this will involve a good deal of reading," he muttered in a low and insecure voice. He was conscious that he and Doc had spent their time in institutions, denied many of the advantages of those, like Cora and the General, who had worked in private families. Nell didn't count. Her child had been a baby.

"Don't worry," said Doc, calmly. "You will sort the rubbish. I will read it. Don't forget, I had plenty of paperwork during my medical years."

The first difficulty, however, was to locate the rubbish in question. Where had the men put it? There was quite a lot, Augustus said, being the day of the move, and the box which had contained the games, the engine and Augustus himself was bright red. That was all the help he could give. Now they must find where the day's refuse had been unloaded. But how? They could, of course, have asked the rats, but they were not to be trusted.

"If only one of us could fly!" said Doc.

The General turned away, offended. And then, as if in answer to their prayers, a large blackbird alighted on the ground nearby.

"Hello again," he said with a slight bow.  He spoke with a familiarity that was for a moment disconcerting to the toys until they recognized the bird whose wing had benefited from Doc's medical training.

"How nice to see you," said Doc. "I trust everything is going well for you—since that tiresome business?"

"Thanks to you," answered the blackbird, flapping his wings up and down in demonstration.

Doc shook his head modestly. "Oh, I didn't really do anything much," he muttered, but Cora was not having this.

"Of course he did!" she said sharply. "We all did! And now you can return the favor!"

The blackbird nodded, somewhat muted by the force of her onslaught. "I thought I heard someone say they wished they could fly."

"Well, yes," said Doc. "The problem is, we need to know where in the dump today's rubbish has been deposited. We would be so grateful for your help."

The blackbird tilted his head first to one side and then the other. "A pleasure," he said, and spreading his wings, he took off.

"And if you see a red box—" called Doc as the bird soared high above them and started to circle the dump.

The toys settled down to wait, but it wasn't long before the blackbird returned. "Northwest of you," he shouted (for all birds have a wonderful sense of direction), "where the oak tree marks the edge of the dump, there are new bags, cardboard boxes that haven't been rained on and one red box in particular. I think that must be it." They called up their thank-yous and asked him to stay, but he shook his head, with an apprehensive glance at Cora. "I don't think I will," he said. "I'm a little bit pushed." And he was gone.

The red box was a sorry sight. It had suffered severely from its passage through the jaws at the back of the garbage truck. The games were torn and ripped and the engine was in three pieces. Augustus shook his head dismally. "Never mind," said Doc. "Just thank your stars they got you out in time. Suppose you'd been lying under the Monopoly box and nobody had seen you."

Augustus nodded, awed by the fate he had escaped.

The General called them to order. "Come on, the lot of you. There's a good deal to be done. We'll tackle this in pairs: Cora and Nell, Doc and Humphrey, and I will help Augustus."

The toys clambered over the bags and got to work. Within half an hour, they had identified four bags that had come from the house, and it was time to start searching. Nell had the hardest job, as it was clear that her partner's heart was not in it.

"The bore of it is, I have to be so careful not to chip my nails," said Cora pitifully, extending her porcelain hands toward the little blue teddy. "It's different for you. You've got such lovely, resilient fur. The slightest thing can crack me."

Nell sighed and opened the nearest bag. It must have come

from the upstairs as it was full of wire coat hangers, discarded cotton wool, and cleaners' covers. Cora leaned forward and snatched up a tiny sample bottle of scent, tipping some of the contents onto her wrists. "Oh," she said, "that's quite nice." She put it into her pocket and stared with more interest into the bathroom debris.

Augustus and the General had selected a bag that seemed to have come from a drawing room or a library and was filled with papers of all sorts. Magazines, bills, torn-up letters, old writing paper and used envelopes were bundled in together. But the more they searched, the more they came across the same problem: everything was addressed to the house on the square. There was nothing to indicate what the new address would be.

Doc and Humphrey had the messier task of dealing with the bag from the kitchen. Rotting vegetables, peelings, tins that were way past their sell-by date and almost-empty bottles that weren't worth keeping were jumbled up in a smelly mess that the bears picked at disdainfully. "There's nothing here," said Humphrey. "We'd better get moving before the rats come. This is Christmas dinner to them." He shuddered.

And then, wedged between an old can opener and a broken dog bowl, Doc suddenly saw a crumpled account from a local shop. He smoothed it out with his paw. It was a list of groceries. In the top left-hand corner was the name of Augustus's family and the address of the house on the square. But on the right it said, "Account address from May 1: Ambleside, Parkway, Deerhurst." He studied it for a moment. It was the clue. With a whoop, he called the others over.

The General took the paper and looked at it in silence. Secretly, he was annoyed that Doc, and not he, had found it, but he resisted the temptation to devalue the discovery and congratulated the bear.

The most marvelous part about it, as they all saw at once, was that the rabbit's family had not moved to another town.

For a moment, Augustus could hardly dare to let it sink in. "But do you know this Parkway?" he asked the others in wonder.

"Certainly we do," said Doc. "The blue truck goes there on Wednesday. That's—" He paused and had started to compute on his paw when Humphrey chimed in. "Tomorrow."

Tomorrow. The blue truck would work its way down Parkway the following morning.

It was time for the General to reveal the next stage of his plan. "This operation will be simple, but it will require a certain amount of nerve. Do you think you're up to that?" He glanced almost severely at Augustus, who did not look as if he were up to anything.

"Of course he is," said Nell.

"Very well. Pay attention." The owl picked up an old plant stake and used it to indicate the various points of the proposed scheme. "The truck will come into Parkway from this end." He started to draw the street in the dirt. "It will be up to those toys riding on the front to find the correct house. On that depends the whole success of the venture. If they fail"—he hesitated for effect—"Augustus may be thrown into the back of the cart. Or on a bonfire."

They all shivered. The rabbit had to sit down.

"Once the house is identified, they will give the signal to Augustus, who will release his string and fall below the cart."

"But what if the men see him?" said Humphrey. "Won't they just pick him up and tie him back on again?"

"Exactly!" said the owl, bringing his stick down with a thwack. "Once on the ground he must crawl, commando-style, under the wheel next to the pavement. But he must be careful to hide behind the wheel and not in front of it."

"Why?" said Cora.

"Because of what would happen when the cart starts forward again," said the owl gravely, and they all fell silent at the thought. Augustus looked very bleak indeed. After a sufficient pause to make his point, the General continued. "Once the truck has gone, the rabbit will spend the day in the gutter. When it is dark, he can make his way to the front door of the house and lie somewhere near the front step—as if he had fallen from a box that was carried inside. As soon as they emerge the following morning, he will be spotted and, with any luck, he should be back with George in time for breakfast. Now"—he looked around—"who wants to accompany Augustus on the journey?" They all raised their hands. "All of you?" said the owl. "You too, Cora? It'll mean getting up early."

"I know," said the doll crossly. "I have been on the trucks before, you know."

"The afternoon runs," muttered Humphrey under his breath.

The owl looked at them. "Well, it'll make for rather a crowded grille," he said. "But then again, it may mean Augustus won't be missed. I'd better come too—in case of last-minute decisions."

The following morning, they all gathered at Doc's orange-box, where Augustus had been his guest for the night, although he clearly hadn't slept a wink. Cora was wearing her usual outfit, but she had chosen a black turban to mark the seriousness of the occasion. Together they set out for the yard and there they found the blue cart ready for an early departure. One by one, they hoisted themselves up and tied their strings, except for Augustus, who was in such a state that he couldn't seem to fasten his. It kept coming undone until he was nearly in tears.

"I don't know what's the matter with me today," he sighed. "I'm all thumbs."

"Stage fright," said Nell. "Let me do it." And she tied the string so that it would come away with a single pull. Once they were fastened, they settled down in silence to wait for the men.

Parkway was on the edge of the town. The houses were large, with wide gardens surrounding them. Cora looked about approvingly. "Oh, this is very attractive," she whispered to Nell.

"I've never lived in the suburbs myself, but I do think one could be quite comfortable here."

As they drove and stopped, drove and stopped, down the long street, the toys anxiously searched for the names on the gates of the houses: ABINGDON and DELANY, WATERFIELD and MANDERLY, until, nearing the corner, they began to fear that they must have missed it. But then the men pushed aside some greenery as they carried the boxes of rubbish from the second last house on the right, and there was the sign. AMBLESIDE, it proclaimed in clear black letters.

"Well," said the General, "this is it."

Augustus reached for the string, but as he took it in his paw, he turned to the others. "I suppose you wouldn't like to come with me," he said. "George is a fine boy. I'm sure he'll take you in."

The General could only shake his head, and the others let Doc speak for them. "Thank you," said the bear gently, smiling at the timid little rabbit. "You're very kind. I know how hard it must be to share a boy—if you are lucky enough to have one. But the rest of us, well, we're too old now, too old and too mended, to start with someone new. You go, and take our very best wishes with you."

"You're quite sure?" said the rabbit with a flicker of relief. The others nodded and smiled, and one or two whispered good lucks could almost be heard above the roar of the engine. Then Augustus pulled the string and fell out of sight beneath the front of the truck.

"I do hope he remembers which way it's going," said Nell under her breath. After that she was silent, as they all were, thinking of the little rabbit beneath the wheels waiting for a return to his old life.

But just as the men had finished and were jumping up on the cab, the door of the house flew open, and out raced a small, fair-haired boy of six or seven years old.

"Please!" he called to the driver. "Please! Wait!" And when he had caught up with them, panting, he spoke. "Please," he said, "have you by any chance come across a small rabbit? In a red

box? Rather an old one, I suppose. In spectacles? You see he was thrown away by accident, and I just wondered if someone might have—" His voice seemed to run out of puff and it was clear that he was having trouble speaking as his eyes had filled with tears. The man scratched his chin.

"I believe we did find one like that, now I come to think of it. Have a look on the front of the truck. I don't know if he's still there." With a gasp of relief the child ran round the cab, but when he looked at the toys he nearly cried again, for of course the rabbit was not among them.

And then he looked down.

"Oh!" he said, and his whole face lit up as if he had swallowed a cup of sunshine. "He *is* here!" Bending down, he scooped up the dusty rabbit and pressed it to his cheek. "Oh, Augustus!" he whispered, and for a moment he couldn't speak at all. Then he returned to the window of the cab. "Thank you." He smiled. "Thank you very much. You see, I should have minded so terribly if he had really been lost."

The men nodded and smiled back, and the truck started to move. George, for obviously it was he, waved and held Augustus up, and already the other toys could see that the rabbit was making a rapid recovery from his unwanted adventures. They watched Augustus and his boy until they turned back into the entrance, out of sight.

"I hope you were speaking for yourself," said Cora in what was perhaps a softer tone than usual. "I'm not too old and mended to start with someone new."

Doc shrugged. "Why didn't you go, then?" he said.

"What use is a little boy to me?" she muttered. "Anyway, as I said, I am not accustomed to the suburbs."

"I was so glad that George came out," said Nell much later that evening, when they were all safely back at the dump and sitting round Cora's hatbox. "Although I'm sure the rest of the General's plan would have worked," she added swiftly, lest the owl should take offense.

"We'll never know if he guessed the right side of the wheel," said the Doc. "And I, for one, am glad his choice wasn't tested."

Even the General nodded at this. "Yes," he said, "he was a nervous little type. I think the scheme was a good one, but all things considered, I was pleased to see him with his boy. . . ." His voice was a little husky as he fell silent, and the others knew he was back on that long-ago platform.

Humphrey smiled. "It's good to see a toy with his child."

"Well," said Cora, "love is a wonderful thing." Singing gently, she raised the lid of the box and started to climb inside. "If anyone is interested," she added as she nestled down into the lavender tissue, "I do not want to be woken early tomorrow."

"Cora's right," said Nell as, later that evening, she and Doc and Humphrey stopped outside her briefcase.

"About what?" snorted Humphrey.

"Love is a wonderful thing."

"Yes," said Doc, and with that, the teddies parted for the night.